CRITICAL BURN

WILDEST SKIES

SEAN MONAGHAN

ALSO BY SEAN MONAGHAN

Find more at the back of this book.

CRITICAL BURN

CHAPTER ONE

The normally gray lunar regolith was scorched and blasted. Sooty, with ejecta from the destruction of a lousy rocket with bad fuel. Streaked with lines from the explosion.

Wreckage lay around the mare.

In his surface suit, a Pirelli, Ed Linklater rolled his shoulders. He'd been out too long, and he was getting tired and grouchy. But someone had to be on the ground to look over this mess.

The sun was low, making shadows long. Another six or so hours and the area would be in darkness. The moon took a month to turn on its axis so sunsets were long. But the light would fail and the temperature would drop. Fast.

Still, it was a good time to be out and looking over the incident site. The long shadows changed the perspective on things.

All around lay pieces of the wreckage. Mostly fist-sized, and smaller. A lot of it was twisted metal and shattered ceramics, but there were a few intact, or almost-intact items. Some electrical cells. PCBs. Tubing.

It was taking some looking into, for sure. What had these people done?

His suit was in good condition, which was saying something. Some of the suits out of Paladan were in rough shape. Nothing that would compromise the user, but plenty of them had been patched up multiple times.

And they could reek. Despite the requirement for undergarments and frequent cleaning, most suits picked up a kind of a fug that just stayed with them.

You learned to live with it.

But this suit was about showroom new. With that *new car smell*, as Ed's father would say. The adhesives and plastics that had gone into the manufacture were still doing their last little bit of curing, exuding volatiles.

His father would understand the situation here too. He'd been involved with railroad management throughout the Midwest and he'd had to attend more than his fair share of derailments and collisions.

This was along those lines, no pun intended. Ed smiled to himself. His father had always loved puns. Especially with the way they would make Ed and his brother Alex groan.

But it was a wreck. That had been unexpected, though Ed was starting to think that it was inevitable.

They were digging so much lithium out of the lunar crust now, it was a wonder that the surface wasn't collapsing. There was money to be made, but sometimes the margins were thin.

And that led to cowboys. No disrespect to cowboys.

But people who were out here running the ragged edge of scraping every last dollar from their operations, well sometimes they took shortcuts.

Suits that made those ageing ones back in Paladan seem positively pristine.

Ships that were cobbled together from parts.

Pilots who believed that courage played as big a part as skill.

Courage did play a role, in a way, but out here, luck could run out faster than a husband caught cheating.

The explosion would have been something to see, that was for sure. Dead silent in the moon's vague excuse for an atmosphere.

Back at Paladan, before setting out in the surface buggy, the team had been over the imagery and other data on the explosion. There was plenty of satellite photography of the site, and a couple of images that had actually captured the explosion itself. Spectacular. Sending rocks and regolith and shattered pieces of the ship hundreds of meters above the surface.

The seismic readings had shown up all over. The equipment was pretty sensitive, and always able to account for legitimate blasting, landings and general activity. The spike had given them triangulation data on the source, which then gave them timings to be able to scour the satellite feed records.

Paladan was the closest base to the explosion site, hence their crew getting called in. Technically it should have been a team from over at Cernan, but they were too far off to drive over. Paladan was just eight kilometers away.

Now it was up to Ed and Giselle to start cleaning up the mess. Looking for human remains with a magnifying glass and tweezers.

Paladan was a smaller base. Only seven people, living in a sub-surface habitat the size of a small house. A compromise on space, and like anyone, Ed did look forward to the opportunity to get out on the surface.

A pity that this time it was down to a tragedy. Even if it was self-inflicted by idiots who shouldn't be allowed off the Earth's surface, it was still a tragedy. They'd still died needlessly.

Ed rolled his shoulders again. Lunar gravity took some getting used to. Even though he'd been on the surface for the last three weeks. Still training himself up as part of the Dashell mission. Some days, he would lean back and look out at the Big Blue Ball and picture the *Cumberland* there in orbit.

Too tiny to see, of course, though Ina, back at the station, had offered to dial in the telescopes and track *Cumberland* as it crossed from the light side and through the terminator.

"Satellites pick up the sun for a little while there," she'd said. "With the night side background, they can show up real well. With a whole lot of magnification your ship will appear as a bright bead of light."

"Some other time," Ed had said. He was very conscious of the vaguest sense of envy from some of the others. There were some long-termers on rotation on the base. Three months on the surface, three months at Taylor or one of the other stations, and three months at home.

The pay was good, but Ed got the feeling from some of them that the routine could grow wearying.

And most everyone worth their salt was envious that he had a place on the Dashell mission. Farthest interstellar flight yet.

Oddly, Giselle was the one from whom he felt that the least. And she'd been on the list for the longest time, ultimately bumped from the crew roster. Not for any particular failing. It would truly be hard to fault Giselle in any capacity. She was one of the most well-rounded people he'd ever worked with. Smart, lateral and with the oddest capacity to suffer fools.

Some might call that last a fault, but a couple of times Ed had been in briefings with her, where some administrator was essentially talking nonsense, riling others up, and Giselle had gone in and asked some clarifying questions, showing genuine interest in the administrator's point of view.

Bringing things around.

"You doing all right there," she said now, through their suit comms. She was about fifteen meters off. They were on a near-channel direct link.

"Sure," Ed said. "Did I seem not?"

"You'd stopped. Gazing up into space."

"Should I not take the opportunity?"

"Of course you should. How's your inspection going?"

"Progressing."

The explosion had left a minor crater in the center. The idiots must have had a decent fuel load aboard. A lot of the wildcatters ran on very low margins. Exactly enough fuel to get them back to orbit and on to their destination and not a milliliter more. Well, maybe an allowance to give them some margin. Setting down could always take a little extra fuel if you had to skip over a couple of boulders. Armstrong had shown that way back when.

But the fuel load on any vessel came at a cost. It took fuel to land, and if you were landing with more fuel than you needed, then you were using up more fuel.

With all the water mines now, and the cometary mining coming online, in-situ fuel made things a whole lot easier. Ships could land almost empty, and fuel up from the ground stores.

But since these people were making illegal landings, they weren't fueling up on the surface. They had to bring their return fuel with them.

And it had cost them their lives.

"Here we are," Giselle said crouching to the surface. "I think I've found their mine."

"The mine?"

"Where they were taking the lithium."

"But here. So close to ground zero?"

He and Giselle had run out in a spiral from the center of the explosion. Ed was conscious that their footprints were leaving marks in the scorched ground, but there was nothing for it. They had to gather as much information as they went. Their suit cameras were recording everything. The computers would be able to rebuild a full three-dimensional image of the site. Even build a scale model.

"It would have been hidden," Giselle said, "were it not for the explosion. I think that it has blasted away the camouflage."

She was kneeling now. Her suit stood out white and orange against the shadowy ground. Her own shadow stretched out in front of her for dozens of meters.

There was something in the ground in front of her.

A dark depression.

Maybe a hole.

CHAPTER TWO

Claude Halbert tried to breathe shallow in the fetid air. This whole thing was just a gyp. He'd been scammed, and he knew it.

He was in the little bunkroom, trying to rest after fourteen hours straight working on the pumps. There was dust in the air, and the lighting was shot.

Should never have come up here. Fool.

He stretched out on the old mattress on the top bunk. Always better to have a top bunk, at least. Even with the clanky old fans, carbon dioxide pooled in the lower areas. Up top the air was always cleaner.

That was at least something.

His eyes were gritty and his mouth was dry.

The supply run had gone awry. Four days back, and already overdue then.

Here he was, stuck in a stinking mine with no way of knowing if he would ever get out.

That payday had seemed brilliant. Enough that he wouldn't have to work for a year or more. He could have gone to Fiji or the Azores and just spent time at the beach with maitais and taquitos.

"Halbert!" Emanuel hollered from somewhere nearby.

There were just the three of them in the mine. Claude, Emanuel Rodriguez and Stacey Grinham. Both of the others were smarter by years than Claude was, and both of them seemed to have an exit plan.

There were just two functional suits.

But the airlock was screwed up. The *Enchanted Whimsy* had exploded on landing, they knew that.

And Emanuel and Stacey were making it look as if they were trying to figure out how they could get all three of them out, but really they were just going to cut and run, he knew it. They would leave him for dead.

"Halbert!" Emanuel was closer.

The habitation section was tiny. Just the narrow bunkroom with four beds, the bathroom which accounted for a whole lot of the stench, a tiny kitchen and a tiny rec room. What a joke this place was.

Most of the space was given over to the mine. Chipping out lithium and other metals from the rock.

A year in Cabo or wherever had seemed like a good trade off.

It wasn't.

"Halbert!" Emanuel was at the bunkroom entrance.

Claude sat up. He coughed. Blinked.

"There you are," Emanuel said. "Lazing around. Come on down. Stacey thinks she'd done a good patch job on suit number six. If we can open up the hatch, we can walk on out of here."

"Where to?"

"Figure that out later. Come on buddy, we're not leaving you behind."

Which was the kind of thing someone like Emanuel would say right before a betrayal.

CHAPTER THREE

E d scanned around the wreckage some more. What a mess.

Giselle was on all fours now, peering into the hole.

"Should I come over?" Ed said.

"Please."

"Should we relay to base?" They were being tracked, but their comms were on a limit to keep things simple. Besides, everyone back at Paladan had their own tasks to work on. Tasha would be on the line, though, any time they asked.

Tasha was the station controller. Quick-witted and always ready to crack open a beer when it had been earned. She'd survived the *Mendocino* station disaster at Ceres, which seemed to give her an odd kind of calm when things started going south. As if she knew she was lucky to still be around, and wasn't going to waste time on worry and regret.

"Open the channel," Giselle said. "And step over. Make sure you get good scans."

"My cameras are operating," Ed said. He reached into the

space in front of his visor and the HUD brought up virtual controls. With his index finger he tapped the bleep back to Paladan so that Tasha would know that they wanted to talk.

"Right here," she said, immediately. She would have a little headset so wherever she was in the station, and whatever she was doing, she could respond right away.

"We have something," Ed said. "A mine entrance."

"Copy that. I see your feeds."

Ed stepped over and stood by Giselle. There was an area of deeper shadow in front of her. Her suit lights shone down onto a hatch set a few centimeters below the general level of the regolith.

There was debris on the far side, where it had been blasted by the explosion.

"It might have had a cap," Giselle said. "Like a piece of plywood with regolith epoxied to the top to make it look like it was just part of the crater floor."

Serenda was a small, minor crater. A few hundred meters across, and shallowed by the incursion of the mare across it.

They were on the moon's limb, with the Earth constantly low to the horizon. Right at the far edge of Oceanus Procellarum. Another hundred or so kilometers and they would have been considered over on the moon's far side.

Ed didn't know all the geological processes behind the various formations of the lunar surface, but he did know that it could be chaotic and messy and even have the geologists scratching their heads.

"I see your hatch there," Tasha said. "They would have used a space to cover it with regolith before they left too."

"You've seen this kind of thing before?" Giselle said.

"Down in the south. Couple of years ago. Water pirates. They had an autonomous bore going on, drilling out the rock and extracting water. A hatch like that. They died too, as it happens."

Ed crouched to the hatchway, opposite Giselle. Ed's suit light activated, shining off the steel.

It was a circle about seventy-five centimeters across, almost perfectly smooth. There were some scrapes and gouges in it. Perhaps from the explosion, perhaps just from general wear and tear.

"Horizontal hatch," Giselle said. "Never much liked those. Too easy to get loose material lodged in the seating."

"Air jets," Ed said. "Around the rim. They'll blow everything clear. And cameras to assess it."

"I know. It still worries me."

Ed leaned back and looked around. The sun continued its steady march toward the horizon. Serenda's crater walls stood like low ramparts. The blackened ground grew darker and more shadowy.

"So, do we open it?" Ed said.

"I guess we have to. Tasha? What's your evaluation?"

"See if it opens," Tasha said. "It forms part of our investigation here. But I don't see any controls. Do you?"

"Perhaps they have to open it from inside," Ed said. He reached out and picked up a loose rock and used it to knock on the hatch. "Open up."

"Not funny," Tasha said.

"There are some controls," Giselle said. "There's a keypad. Pretty dusty and gritty."

"Keypad? That implies a code."

"Yes it does."

"Can you override it?"

"The codes we have are for legitimate installations. Something like this is going to be off-grid. No chance of breaking the code. We have to come back with a cutting wheel and a pry bar."

"Try a code," Ed said. "You never know."

As part of their training they'd been taut a series of back-channel codes that could jailbreak a whole bunch of systems. Twenty-two digits each, with specific timings. You had to enter ten digits, pause for five seconds, enter the next ten, then pause again before entering the final two digits. High-level security stuff specific to their work. There was no sense in dying because there was no way to access a computer or to open a door.

Use, though, was strictly limited and monitored. They could use it to save their lives, but there would still be endless screen-work after. Dozens of forms to fill out. Days' worth.

Giselle muttered something under her breath. She started tapping in a code.

The keypad's digits were big enough to easily press with a suit's gloved finger.

A tiny burst of distant static jabbed through Ed's helmet.

"Hear that?" Giselle said.

"Yes."

The static came again. High-pitched. Annoying.

Ed leaned back as Giselle kept punching in the code. Ed activated his HUD by putting his hand up in front of his face. He brought up the radio system diagnostics. Ran a quick check.

"External interference?" he said. "Tasha? Are you hearing this?"

"Hearing what?"

"Static. We got a blast of it."

"Like?"

"Like someone with a busted mic maybe? Or as if my helmet's speakers are broken."

"They're not?"

"I'm hearing you just fine. I ran a suit check on the radio system and it seems nominal."

"Copy that. Let me grab your recording here and see what it is."

Giselle was still punching in the number. The sun continued to set.

"We might need some more equipment out here," Ed said. "One of the borers, perhaps. Maybe a—"

The static came again. Louder.

"Ouch," Giselle said. Then she cursed.

She leaned back from the code pad.

"Lost count?" Ed said.

"That's really disruptive."

"Can you find the source? Tasha's not getting it."

"I heard." Giselle looked away toward their buggy, parked at the edge of the debris field. They had tools stowed aboard. Perhaps even something that might pry open the hatch.

The static came again.

"Maybe there's still an active piece of equipment in the wreckage," Giselle said. "Maybe it's just an automated connection signal. Some little actuator or pump that's become detached from its housing and is trying to calibrate."

"Could be." But the static had started up when Giselle began tapping at the code pad.

"Let's run a scan," Giselle said, standing. She reached up in front of her visor and began operating the virtual space there. "If I can scan for frequencies, maybe it will show up. Maybe it's just something tuned in badly. Maybe even a satellite."

"I believe that it's local," Ed said. "Right here with us."

"Right, Tasha's not hearing it." Ed lay out on the regolith and leaned in close to the hatch.

"What are you doing?" Giselle said.

"Trying something. Don't laugh." Ed placed the side of his helmet down against the hatchway.

"If that thing opens," Giselle said, "you're going to tumble in."

"Maybe." Ed took the rock again and he banged it twice against the hatch. The sound was loud in his helmet. Direct connection.

Then two muted, distant bangs came back.

"Uh-oh," Ed said.

CHAPTER FOUR

Down in the little machine shop, Claude started pulling on the suit legs. The colors didn't match. The left leg was orange and white, and the right leg was a kind of indeterminate color somewhere around brown and khaki and tan. Depended on the light. He could see glistening fibers within it, where the outer layer had worn through.

The whole thing stank of age and mold and urine. Like a dog's pee. And here Claude was sticking his legs into it.

Stacey was busy at one of the benches. She had her suit on, just without the helmet. Her legs matched. And matched the top, above the waist ring.

Emanuel's suit was more beaten up than Stacey's, but was still pristine compared to Claude's.

"Long time since I've been in a suit," Claude said. He leaned back against one of the workbenches. There were tools and parts scattered around. In a way it didn't look much different to the debris field above on the satellite photos that Stacey had managed to cadge from the system.

"It's been six weeks," Emanuel said.

"Like I said." When the three of them had set down for the change out, they'd dressed in decent transfer suits. Little life support packs, enough for an hour or so, with no toileting or sustenance settings. No HUD.

They'd just walked from the *Enchanted Whimsy*, their little packet freighter ship that had set down a hundred meters or so from the access hatch. Once inside, there were three gaunt crew waiting on the other side of the air lock. The three helped Claude, Emanuel and Stacey out of the suits and donned them themselves. Departed with barely a word.

Leaving the three new arrivals to their own devices.

Six awful weeks, with months still to come.

Money. What a terrible motivator.

And now the *Enchanted Whimsy* had blown itself apart right above the hidden hatch.

Emanuel lifted the suit's torso toward Claude.

"Duck," Emanuel said. "Wriggle in."

Claude ducked, and bent his head to get under the waist ring. This section of the suit was the worst. Puffy like it should be in places, but kind of caved in in others. As if the thermal insulation and protective layers and whatever smart technologies lay within had collapsed and broken down like some old newspaper turning to dust.

"I had a nice job before this," Claude said as his head came out through the neck ring. He wriggled his arms down the sleeves. His left thumb caught up on a tear in the interior fabric. He pulled his hand back.

"A nice job?" Stacey said without turning. She was looking at one of the old helmets. Above her, ducts and conduits lined the rock wall. All of this was pretty makeshift, really. Burrowed through layers of the rock illicitly, and then fitted out fast and lazy.

"It was a nice job," Claude said. "Dolthick Lake Environmental Officer. I could get out on the boat and scoop up weed and put up signs to stop people tromping over gecko nests and grab a cheap soda from the machine at the park office. That was the life."

"What happened, then?"

He'd already told them, on the flight out from Earth, but as a group they'd never gelled. Never really fitted in. The three of them just needed cash.

"Little divorce, and I lost my job. Lost the house. Lost the kids."

"You got kids?" Emanuel said.

"Two of them. Six and eight." Claude had told them all this. At least he'd hoped that coming out here, he would at least have some company to take his mind off the flaming remains of his life back home. Hadn't happened.

"You should be there looking after them," Emanuel said.

"Yeah. All this..." Claude waved his hand around the machine shop with its barely functional set up. Enough to keep the boring and processing machines operating, and little else.

A distant clang came along one of the pipes above Claude's head. Immediately came another.

With his now-gloved hand, Claude picked up a wrench and banged the pipe twice.

"Hey!" Stacey said, turning. "Don't wreck the place."

"It's already wrecked," Claude said. "We have no transport out of here. You two are ready to abandon it in your perfect suits and me, well, I'm just chancing it."

More quiet clangs. Three. Then another three.

Staring at Stacey, Claude whacked the pipe again. Three times, then three more times.

"Might be someone topside," he said as fury gripped Stacey's face. "Someone trying to get in touch. Maybe someone who's here to help."

"No one's coming to help."

"Maybe they are. You don't know that. You should pull down some more satellite imagery and see if—"

Another set of clangs came through the pipe. Sharper. A little louder. And a sequence he knew.

Clang clang-clang clang... clang.

"Don't," Stacey said.

Still staring at her, Claude reached above and answered.

Clang clang.

CHAPTER FIVE

S till leaning against the hatch with his helmet, Ed banged again. Three times.

A moment later, three distant, muted bangs came back.

He tried a pattern. *Bang bang bang,* pause *bang bang bang.*

And the same came back.

Could just be an echo, though. Maybe a reverberation through the metal of whatever structure lay below.

Something different then.

Ed tapped out, *Bang bang-bang bang... bang.*

A moment, then the response.

Bang bang.

An age-old call and response.

"There's someone down there," Ed said. "How's your Morse Code?"

"My what?"

Morse code had long gone the way of the dinosaurs. Even

the military didn't teach it anymore. So how were they going to communicate with the people below?

"Morse?" Tasha said.

"This just got bigger," Ed said. "There are people down there. Well, at least one person."

"You know this how?"

"Responded to my taps."

"You heard taps?"

"Helmet against the hatch. Conduction."

"Understood."

"We need to get the hatch open then," Giselle said.

"Yes." Unless there wasn't an airlock below. Opening the hatch would compromise whatever facility lay beneath the surface here.

No. There had to be an airlock. Whatever system these people were using, they needed to be able to safely seal their installation. They might be wildcatters, but that didn't mean they were idiots.

"Tasha?" Ed said. "Can you run through the radio spectrums from our suits? See if we can't pick up their signal. Best way to talk to them."

"Trying now."

"Thanks."

Giselle crouched again to the code pad. She wiped at it with her glove.

"Thought there might be a connection here," she said. "You know, maybe even just an audio jack."

Despite the prevalence of wireless comms, nothing beat a physical connection for communications and control.

"Nothing?" Ed said.

"Nope."

"Tasha?"

"There's nothing," Tasha said. "No radio signal coming from that facility at all. I would think it is abandoned."

"But someone signaled back."

"Echoes."

"Nope. Different patterns."

"Copy that. I'll run through the spectrums again. See what we can find."

"Thanks. We'll keep working on it here."

"Good."

Giselle leaned back on her haunches and looked at Ed. He could see his own suit reflected in her curved visor. Like those old first landing photographs.

"Do we have to drill then?" Ed leaned back too. "Or get some sounding equipment out here and map whatever they've got below?"

"I like that idea." Giselle shifted her weight. "Perhaps there's another entry. That would make sense, really. If they're shifting out ingots or raw rock, a vertical shaft here likely isn't very efficient."

"Sure." Ed stood and looked around the debris field again. "Maybe, though, they use cannisters and haul them up with a winch."

It would be near-impossible to look over the field and tell a winch from a servo motor from a control box. Most of the debris was too small to really make any kind of identification. Twisted and torn metal and plastic and ceramic.

"We could get a contact mic," Giselle said. "Tape it to the hatch and listen in."

"How would we talk to them?"

"Fair point. Maybe we drill a controlled hole in the hatch and lower a full mic and speaker set through the hole. Tasha, would we have something like that on inventory?"

"Probably," Tasha said. "I can go look. But there are a whole lot of other issues there. Such as sealing the hole behind the drill?"

Ed imagined a drill bit equipped with everything they needed. Microphone and speaker. The bit could self-seal behind itself and relay the details.

"We could tent over the hatch," Giselle said.

They had inflatable micro-habitats that could be set up for emergencies or rest periods or even to catch a little sleep. Self-healing, with folded carbon fiber flaps on the top to protect from micrometeorites.

But they were designed as a single unit. Floor, walls and ceiling. No access to the ground below.

Opening to the regolith would be tricky. No way to really ensure a good seal.

"You have a tent in your buggy?" Tasha said. "Wait, yes you do. You'd need to cut out the bottom and bond it into the hatch seating."

They were getting too complicated here.

"Do we need to worry?" Ed said. "Eventually they're going to come out, aren't they?"

"Probably," Tasha said. "But in my estimation, we still need to get into whatever is down there. It's clearly associated with the destroyed vessel, so we're going to find useful information."

"Copy that."

Ed stepped back from the hatch.

"We need surveys," he said. "We need all the recent data on Serenda Crater. We need to run that through analysis and figure out any changes over recent times. Say two years. Parse that data down and see what's changed. When the hatch was installed. And if there was anything else installed at the same time. Like an escape hatch or a service space."

Ed peered at the distant crater wall. He started walking. Scanning as he went.

"Maybe," he said, "there's a cave? Do those occur in craters?"

"This crater's been filled by a lava flow," Giselle said. "And the caves are really lava tubes. But still, it's hard to know."

"Lava tubes are rare," Tasha said. "I mean, there are hundreds upon hundreds, but only a certain percentage are occupiable. And when you consider the entire surface of the moon, something close to forty million square kilometers, well... sorry, didn't mean to give a science lesson."

"It's all right," Ed said. "All the data counts. Besides, I'm thinking that if there was another exit, then why would they bang back at me? They must know that the ship was destroyed. To my mind they should have just gone ahead and left their facility."

"Maybe they don't have suits," Giselle said.

"Why would they not have suits?" Tasha said. "Surely that's a basic standard for any lunar facility. Even one that's running off the books and under the radar."

"I see what you did there. You just mean 'illegally', don't you?"

"Yes I do."

"They run on a minimum," Ed said. "But yeah, you would think that suits would be right up near the top of their inventory. My question, though, would be, where would they go? They're not supposed to be here. Their service vessel has been destroyed. Paladan is the closest base and we're eight kilometers off. The ground is not too rough, but still, walking that distance in a suit would take it out of anyone. Assuming that they could navigate to us. Then there would be no guarantee that they could even get inside."

Ed kept looking across the debris field as he walked. Was

there another hatchway? Was there a service door in the crater wall? Would that even be possible? Wouldn't it take a whole lot of drilling and blasting?

"We'd let them in," Tasha said. "Of course."

"They wouldn't know that," Giselle said. "People like that, their thoughts revolve around how everyone is out to get them. Kindness from others doesn't figure into it. Wouldn't occur to them. But all that said, perhaps they have a vehicle anyway."

"Perhaps," Ed said. "But still where to go? And if this is their only exit then how would they get a vehicle up and out?"

"Right. And we'd have to assume that their entire operation is below ground. Why would they even need a vehicle?"

"For emergencies," Tasha said.

"But they don't think like us," Ed said. "They run at the finest of margins. Pushing the limits."

They were talking it out too much. They needed data.

They needed to get those people out.

From the responses, clearly they were in trouble.

CHAPTER SIX

C laude carried his helmet and followed the other two through some of the narrow bored corridors. He was hungry. More cables and conduits festooned the walls, close to the ceiling. Claude wasn't tall, but he had to bend sometimes to fit under the drapes of the utilities.

"Where are we going?" he said. The walls were undressed rock. There was talk that all occupiable sections needed to be sealed with some kind of coating. The rock wasn't necessarily porous, but then, it didn't take much porosity to bleed air out of a section.

"Load-out bay," Stacey said. "I brought up one of the ore carts. Think that I might have adapted it for surface travel."

The ore carts ran down into the bowels of the rough mine. They hauled the ore from the face, but up to the processor which physically and chemically munched everything down essentially to dust and pooped out ingots of various metals. Mostly lithium, but there was some gold and silver too. A little platinum.

Claude had only once seen the mine itself. A vast chamber as big as two cathedrals side by side. Dark, since the machines didn't need much light. The sounds of them working echoed eerily through the chamber.

The miners trundled slowly around, working out and down, chipping away the chamber's sides, and loading the rock into the ore carts.

It was all basically autonomous. The three humans were only on site to keep an eye on things and perform maintenance when the machines couldn't do it themselves. Sometimes there was some problem-solving.

A week back, one of the miners had decided that it should be digging vertically and started chewing itself a hole toward the center of the moon. They'd lowered Claude down on a rope to stand on the back of the thing and drill a hole into the case and reset the miner.

Fun times like that.

But the ore carts themselves had limited speed and weren't like a passenger vehicle. Really just a tub on wheels, with a little electric motor, stiff wheels and strong suspension.

"How did you adapt it?" Claude said.

"I tore off the ore hopper and welded on some seats. I goosed the motors with some extra motors from another cart, and chained in a trailer so we can haul any gear we need."

"Did you make space for me?"

"There's always space for you," Stacey said.

But when they came into the load-out bay, it was clear that the cart only had two seats. There was more space on the chassis, but it would be tough to have to hold on.

"Two seats," Claude said.

"I'm going to weld on another one. The job isn't finished yet."

They came to the load-out bay's airlock. Claude peered through the window in the hatch.

The load-out bay was the size of two school classrooms end to end, with the floor from halfway along rising toward the ceiling as a ramp.

The flat floor was filled with pallets ready to truck up to the surface and load into the *Enchanted Whimsy*.

Except that the ship wasn't coming.

Or, at least, it was already on the surface, just that it was in billions of pieces and would never leave again.

Above the angled ramp section was a hydraulically-supported plate. A disguise for the mine, the same way that the habitat-section hatch was disguised, with glued regolith.

The load-out bay worked mostly in vacuum. The plate had a good seal, but it was pretty huge. Plenty of opportunity for it to fail.

When Claude had been driving the little lift tractors to load up pallets of ore, he had always been wearing a station suit. Simple, and hosed and powered from the tractor itself. But that suit had been in better shape than the one he was wearing now.

When the ship would touch down, the ramp would open and Ed and the others would drive their tractors up and load the ship's cargo bay. They had it down to an art. Fast and efficient. A good rotor. They could load thirty pallets in little more than an hour.

And the ship came by every week, more or less.

Claude donned his helmet and locked it into the neck ring. He ran check on his forearm display, trying to check the suit's integrity.

It kept glitching and not giving him data.

"I'll partially evacuate," Stacey said, with the airlock's

internal hatch closed. There was little space for the three of them in their suits.

"This is a crazy plan," Claude said.

"Agreed," Stacey said. "But it's better than no plan."

"We could call for help."

"We'd be thrown in the klink straight away," Emanuel said. "Though that might be a step up from the accommodations here."

Claude's suit creaked and expanded around him as Stacey pumped the air out of the lock.

Listening hard, Claude didn't get any sense of air leaving the suit. No whistling or whines.

"We're at fifty kilopascals," Stacey said. "Half atmospheric pressure. Not quite the summit of Everest, but you might be noticing? I mean if the suit was leaking."

"Doesn't seem to be."

"All right then. I'm going to continue pump the air out."

"If it's all right with you," Emanuel said.

Claude considered a moment. The underground habitat was sealed and relatively safe. With the two of them gone, there would be supplies for a good month and a half.

But then what?

"It's all right with me," Claude said. "Pump it all out."

CHAPTER SEVEN

In the blast field in Serenda crater, Ed kept scanning. Kept looking for clues about what might be a mine below them.

It had to be on pretty small scale. But then, there were occupants. The first duty was to them.

"Tasha," Ed said. "I'm looking over the far crater wall. The eastern side. I don't see anything that might constitute an access point. But can you look at the western wall imagery? It's in shadow now, so I can't see a thing. Especially with the sun's glare."

"I can pull up satellite images. Old surveys."

"Good, thanks."

"Surely," Giselle said, "someone would have noticed them establishing this place."

"Forty million square kilometers," Ed said. "Can't be watching it all the time."

"But the blasting. The drilling. I mean, they didn't just find this hole, did they? They dug it out an installed the hatch. I'm looking at it here, and there's packing grout around the seating here. Fill." Giselle was still kneeling by the hatch.

"It could be old," Ed said. Perhaps they've just commandeered an existing facility. I mean, in the early days when just about everyone was wildcatting out here, there were an awful lot of bases established."

"That would be on record."

"Most likely." In the early days, even with the lack of regulation, people still registered. "Tasha, do you see any records?"

"Nothing," Tasha said. "Serenda Crater has never been occupied."

Ed kept walking, kept scanning the crater wall for something. Anything.

"So this is recent," Giselle said. "Like months, perhaps. Maybe only weeks."

"Agreed," Ed said "Perhaps this was their first production collection."

"Right. A decent load of refined ore, perhaps switching out the ground crew and skedaddling."

"*Skedaddling*?" Tasha said.

"That's a word."

"I know."

"But still," Giselle said. "Wouldn't their drilling, if that's what they were up to, wouldn't it show on the seismics?"

"Maybe," Ed said. "Maybe not. There's an awful lot of noise out here. They might have even been able to time any blasting with blasting at other locations."

"But triangulation. That's how we ended up here, right?"

"Sure, but it would mean someone would have to be looking. Part of why we ended up here was the distinct nature of the explosion. Above ground, so there was a different quality to it all."

Ed noticed something ahead. A break in the scorching.

Of course, with striding across the area, he was messing with the scorch marks.

The break was actually a line. As if someone had come out specifically to draw it. Like the chalk line sprinkled across a speedway track when the cars did a rolling start.

"Got something," he said.

"Should I come look?" Giselle said.

"Let me look it over first."

"What is it?"

"Just a straight line. It seems weird in the context of everything here being so jumbled and chaotic."

"Copy that."

Wreckage lay around the line. Some of it right across. A sheet of laminated paper with instructions. A board with a dozen switches across it. Torn and twisted plating.

Ed stopped just a few centimeters from the line. It was a hollow in the regolith. Not like rille. More like a long, narrow trench. A few centimeters deep and about as wide. It stretched about six meters.

Ed carefully walked to one end of it.

"There's something under here," he said.

"Do we need to get a probe?"

"Yes." They had various aluminum spikes they could use to stab into the regolith to check on surface consistency and strength.

"I'll call over the vehicle," Giselle said. "Yeah?"

"Yes." They'd parked the buggy a hundred meters beyond the edge of the blast radius so they could get a better picture of things without disturbing the surface too much. That was about done. They needed to move with speed at this juncture.

Giselle walked toward Ed. He saw the buggy lurch and start forward from the distance. The buggy came quickly.

"I see the line," Giselle said. "That's another hatch?"

"Another hatch?" Ed said. "It's all the wrong shape."

Giselle stood in the middle of the line.

Ed stepped over it and walked back toward her.

"It doesn't feel any different underfoot."

"You just—" Giselle stopped as Ed jerked.

The ground moved under his feet.

And he was descending.

CHAPTER EIGHT

Claude clung to the makeshift seat that Stacey had last-moment zip-tied to the hotrod ore cart's chassis.

She and Emanuel were just fine up front. Easy chairs stolen from the mine's little rec room. Welded in.

Apparently, she'd been working on this from the moment she'd realized that the *Enchanted Whimsy* had blasted itself to smithereens.

While Claude, if he was honest with himself, had sat around moping.

Well, kind of vaguely trying to figure a way out of the mess, but that was not really his specialty at all. He'd just come out here chasing the money.

Amazing to think that it used to cost millions to put someone into orbit or on the moon. Millions or billions. And now, it was so simple that people would pay you to ride out.

And still make money themselves. Lots of money. Virtual slave labor.

Especially when you ended up in a situation like Claude's.

"You're going to be fine," Stacey said. "Just hold on."

"Remember it's lunar gravity," Emanuel said. "You can't get hurt."

Which was such a fallacy. Plenty of ways to get hurt. Plenty of ways to get dead.

It was fine for the two of them, sitting up front with their welded seats and makeshift safety harnesses strapping them to those seats.

"Why do you dislike me so?" Claude said.

"Huh?" Emanuel said.

"He means me," Stacey said. "And don't take it personally, Claude. I dislike everyone."

"She does."

"Clam it up, Emanuel. Listen, Claude. Things went south for me a long time ago. Look where I've ended up. Trying to come up with a few coins to actually live a life. Trying to stay out of the way of the sharks who would eat me up. Your life has been going infinitely better than mine. And I'm just bitter and angry."

"Infinitely is a big word," Emanuel said.

"Clam it!" Stacey turned around in the seat, her suit wrinkling. Claude couldn't see her face through her helmet's visor.

"Claude," she said. "I was going to weld in a seat for you, but timing. We wouldn't be leaving now except that we've been discovered. So make do and hold on."

"All right," Claude said. He had little choice really. While the money was supposedly going to be good, they were still operating an illegal mine. They could still face consequences for that. Serious, jail-time type consequences.

"Here we go," Stacey said. "Hold on."

Above and in front of them, the big load-out bay hatch jerked. It began moving down. Heading for the ramp.

There was someone standing there.

Coming down on the hatch.

CHAPTER NINE

As the ground moved under his feet, Ed stepped back. He held his arms out to steady himself.

Through his feet, he could feel the vibrations of the mechanisms operating. Was it big hydraulics, or chains or big cogs?

The ground was tipping. Looking around, he could see the margins of the area. The rim of the opening. Maybe five or so meters across, and maybe fifteen meters long. It was tipping down slowly, and he was near the leading edge.

He took another step back.

"Get off of there," Giselle said. "If that tips vertically, it could dump you into a shaft."

"Could," he said, bending to peer ahead.

There was a lit opening. A floor there, stacked with loaded plastic crates, strapped to loading pallets. A lift tractor parked right by one.

"Looks like they were preparing to load out," Ed said.

"You need to move."

"No, it's fine. I can see how this is going to work. This is a loading ramp."

On the rock sides, there were vertical curved grooves that the mechanism would ride to stay true and even. Perhaps the thing was sprung, and used cables to pull it down. This loading bay might be perpetually run in vacuum.

He started getting a better view of the interior. If the ramp's tilt took it to the floor of the bay, then the ramp would end up at about thirty degrees. Steep, but not so steep that he couldn't stay upright.

And easy enough for that little tractor to drive up with its pallet loads.

Then he spotted another vehicle. It looked like an old lunar rover. Like the ones those early Apollo astronauts had hauled up with them so they could explore a little farther. Four wheels at the corners, a little chassis with two seats.

No. Three seats.

Occupied.

Three people in suits.

Staring right at him.

The ramp continued to descend.

Probably at around twenty degrees now. Pretty soon he would be able to step off the end and onto the floor. Just a couple more meters.

Actually, he could probably jump from here safely.

But he stayed where he was. He lifted his right hand and waved, with his hand vertical.

None of them waved back.

The one on Ed's right was working on the vehicle's controls. Almost frantic.

"People down here," Ed said.

Then it occurred to him that he was standing almost right in front of their vehicle. If they decided to drive up they would run right over him.

The ramp was now at about twenty-five degrees. Not far to go and the forward lip—which was the line he'd seen from the surface—would reach the floor.

And they didn't necessarily need to wait for it to touch down. Those wheels were close to a meter across. They could easily negotiate small obstacles.

Ed looked up.

Giselle was there, looking over the lip of the hole, just her helmet and shoulders visible.

"Ed?" she said.

"Yeah. Looks like they're loaded up and ready to go."

"Go where?"

"Good question. We need to find their frequency and ask th—"

The vehicle lurched ahead.

Ed stumbled.

The vehicle was quick. It bounced over the ramp's rim.

Turned a fraction.

Missed him by centimeters.

Turning, Ed watched the vehicle speed up the ramp.

The occupant in the rear seat had turned to watch him back.

CHAPTER TEN

Claude clung on. The modified ore cart bounced and shook its way across the crater floor.

How could the vehicle be moving so fast? When he'd worked on them in the mine, they'd always been slow thing. They reminded him of chugging paddle-wheelers on the Mississippi. Places to be, but no particular rush to get there.

Now they had to be doing at least twenty miles an hour. Maybe thirty.

"Where are we headed?" Emanuel said.

"Old facility I was at a year back," Stacey said. "It's about sixty, seventy miles off."

"Hours to get to, then?"

"Yep."

"Will out suits hold out?"

"Yours and mine will be just fine."

"Thanks," Claude said. "Thanks a lot."

He'd watched behind, over the trailer, as they'd ascended the ramp. Some guy there in a suit, watching him.

Whoever he was he'd found the mine. Realized that the ramp was a way in.

And then there had been another one standing up on the regular surface, watching too.

And not far beyond that one, there had been a lunar buggy.

"People," Claude said.

"We knew they'd found us," Stacey said. "You saw the guy on the ramp?"

"I think you almost ran him down."

The ore cart bumped and jerked. Despite the small guards, rooster tail sprays of the loose lunar dust launched from the wheels.

Some of it was drifting onto Claude's suit.

"Hey Claude," Emanuel said. "Your suit's going to be just fine too. If you notice any issues tell me and I'll wrap you up in a bubble."

"Great, thanks." Claude hadn't even realized that their mine had survival bubbles on inventory. Not that the inventory records were any good anyway.

The bubble was just a multi-layered, meter-wide sphere of vinyl and other materials with a sealable entrance and a port for air exchange. A simple way to keep someone alive in vacuum.

It did leave them extraordinarily dependent on someone outside the bubble to move them to safety.

They were approaching the crater wall. Moving real fast now.

Kind of scary. Kind of crazy driving.

But then, it was a desperate situation, wasn't it?

Claude had a bad feeling that they were just delaying the inevitable.

"Hey," he said. "What's this other facility?"

"Another mine," Stacey said. "Abandoned. You'll love it."

"I'll love anything that's not bouncing around like this."

Stacey and Emanuel laughed.

The crater wall began to loom.

CHAPTER ELEVEN

E d climbed into the buggy next to Giselle. She was at the controls and eased them forward.

The buggy was a six-wheeler, with a small cab with simple doors, but in behind lay a tiny shirt-sleeve space. Kind of like a little motorhome. There was a single-person airlock between the cab and the interior.

"They're moving really fast," Giselle said. "Thirty-two miles an hour."

"Car chase on the moon, huh?"

"Funny. But I don't know that we can actually keep up."

"Are we running on a restrictor plate?" Some of the NASCAR ethanol races still used those to moderate the speed of stockcars.

"Our normal speed is fifteen kilometers per hour. That lets us get plenty of places in reasonable time."

"It's not like we really have far to go."

Paladan was a research and training base. Non-commercial.

The buggy took them out to various features and small, autonomous installations for training purposes.

This jaunt out to Serenda Crater was the longest Ed had taken. He didn't know about Giselle.

"So they're going to get away from us, are the?"

"Not likely. We can track them easily enough. Get some over-head guidance."

The other vehicle continued to shrink in the distance. Probably moving twice their speed.

"It seems to me," Ed said, "that they're heading east. Into darkness."

"So we can track their lights."

"How long can we stay out?"

"We'll be able to catch them."

"Not at this rate. What is the duration rating on the buggy? Thirty-six hours?"

"Eight days." Giselle reached up and knocked on the airlock door. "Why do you think it has bunks? And I think eight days is just the manufacturers covering themselves. Pretty sure we could manage twelve comfortably."

"After twelve days, I'm going to be pretty sick of dried food."

"Buddy, you want to go to deep space. On missions that take months. If you can't do twelve days on the lunar surface, then I take pity on you. And your future crewmates."

Ed laughed.

It seemed a strange kind of banter to be having while they were chasing another vehicle across the blasted lunar plains.

The other vehicle turned. It started tracking across to the left.

"What's going on there, do you think?" Ed said.

"Maybe they didn't think this through very well. I think that they don't know where to cross the crater wall."

"Interesting. Can they? I mean, we drove easily enough through a gap. There are plenty of gaps."

"I think they're making for one." Giselle pointed.

Ed peered forward.

"I kind of see it," he said.

"Changing course now."

CHAPTER TWELVE

The ore cart bounced something terrible up the slope of the break in the crater wall. A couple of times the jerking around almost threw Claude from his makeshift seat.

How had Stacey been able to pimp the ore cart so much in just a couple of days? He'd only known her briefly, and she was pretty standoffish, but it had always been clear that she knew her way around machines.

"Hang on, Claude," she said as the ore cart progressed up the slope. "It's going to get bumpy ahead."

"It's already bumpy."

Emanuel laughed. "Fella, you don't know what you're in for."

Claude stretched up as best he could in his suit and tried to see ahead. Sure enough, the ground grew rougher. The slope was steeper than the ramp out of the mine, and it looked as if over the eons, rocks had been regularly falling from the open sides around the opening. It was as if they were heading up into a pass. A notch in the crater wall.

The next bump almost threw him from the seat.

Emanuel reached around to help steady him.

"Thanks," Claude said. It was unexpected.

"Sure. Hey, Stacy, whyn't you slow it down a little?"

"They're following us." Stacey stayed focused on driving the vehicle ahead.

"Sure," Emanuel said. "I can see them from here. And we're leaving them in our dust. Progressing slowly through the pass won't make any difference. They're not going to catch us. Especially once we're up and over the rim. They won't have a sightline. And we'll be in shadow."

"We won't."

"Sure we will. The sun is setting. The crater wall stands up about, what, five, ten meters above grade? We'll be in its shadow for ages. Maybe even if we do get out of it, the sun will have set. After all, we're driving away from the sun."

"Not at an appreciable speed," Claude said. "Sunset takes a week from high noon to darkness."

"Yeah, yeah."

"He's right," Stacey said. "Also, when we are in shadow, I'll have to run with lights."

"We have lights?" Emanuel said.

"Oh, yeah. Tore them from the mine processing conveyor's ceiling. You know the big thirty-thousand lumen LEDs?"

"Right."

Claude clung on as they continued to ascend. The ride was more even. Stacey had slowed the ore cart.

Claude looked back.

The other vehicle was still coming along behind them. Losing ground, but still it reminded him of a movie he'd seen with his father when Claude had been about ten. *The Mummy of Cairo*. The hero, Shaw Constant, had broken into a tomb and whichever curse had driven the mummy to make pursuit. The mummy had been slow. Shuffling. Shaw had laughed.

But the mummy was relentless. Never slept. Never stopped. Just kept walking toward Shaw. Wherever he went.

The ending had been terrifying. A battle in Rome, and Shaw barely able to escape with his life.

And as Claude looked back, it was clear that these people were in a vehicle a thousand times better than the one he'd hitched himself to.

This was not going to go well.

As if to confirm what he was thinking—or had he jinxed it!—the ore cart shuddered and came to a stop.

Stacey cursed.

"Huh," Emanuel said. "Guess we walk from here?"

Stacey cursed some more and called him some names questioning his parentage and his prowess.

"Yeah," he said. "Fair call, maybe."

"Shut up," Stacey said. "Get off your butt and come help me fix this pile of junk."

Claude watched the other vehicle.

Still coming.

Relentless.

CHAPTER THIRTEEN

E d peered ahead through the buggy's forward window. The other vehicle might have come to a stop.

They'd gotten partway up a vague kind of ramp on the crater's edge. It looked almost like a river's alluvial fan back on Earth, but there were no water processes here to create such a landform. Still, rocks and sand and dust tended to move down, so there was some process going on.

"They've stopped," Giselle said. "We might make some gains here."

The buggy continued to hum as it drove across the crater floor. Fifteen miles an hour. The people from the mine could probably run faster across the surface.

"Where were they heading do you think?" Ed said. "There's a whole lot of nothing around here." Serenda was a minor crater, out in the mare.

"There are other stations," Giselle said. "Might be they have their eyes on one of those."

"We were the closest, though."

"But they don't know us. Maybe they have friends somewhere else. Tasha, are you still on the line here?"

"Yes I am."

"Can you see if you can locate any other base in the direction they're heading? Or maybe a waiting ship? Some reason they might be heading south east."

"Looking now."

Giselle kept driving. Ed took a sip from the drink tube in his suit, surprised by how dry his mouth had become.

Concentrating on other things.

Ed pulled up one of the buggy's console displays and used the onboard cameras to zoom in on the other vehicle.

The three occupants had climbed out. They were moving around the vehicle.

"Suit's don't match," Ed said.

"So?" Giselle said.

"Implies that it's a makeshift operation. Ratty and rough."

"I think we already knew that."

"Sure, but it's intriguing to see it on display so clearly."

It was hard to tell what kind of a vehicle they had out there. It had big disk wheels with little tread. A two-wheeled trailer. A flat kind of chassis. The seats looked as if they didn't quite match.

"It's an ore cart," Ed said. "They've modified it to run on the surface. Taken off the hopper tray and welded on seats."

"Innovative."

"Desperate, I think. They lost their transport out of the mine, so they've had to figure out another way."

"Yes. I wish they had just come straight to us, though."

"I know it."

On the display, one of the suited figures had lain right down on the ground and was working at the base of the makeshift vehicle's chassis.

Tasha came over the comms.

"I have a precis of other bases in the area," she said. "Nothing for over a hundred and thirty kilometers. There is an old Artemis landing site a little closer, but that's been there for decades and really there's just the landing stage and a few pieces of equipment lying around. It was one of the first tests so they didn't even set up a habitat in place. Nothing these people could use there."

"So they're planning on traveling a hundred and thirty klicks?" Ed said.

"No. That nearest base is a small private scientific outpost. Three staff running assays on the Oceanus material. They're a satellite of a bigger outfit another sixty kilometers off. But there is an abandoned habitat around one hundred and forty-five kilometers from your position. One of the early Indian landing sites. They dug up regolith and put in a multi-chambered habitat. I'm looking for the schematics now so I can get a better impression of it."

"A hundred and forty-five?"

"That's correct."

"And their transport has already broken down just a couple of klicks from their departure point."

"Right," Giselle said. "But I have a feeling that it might just be teething trouble. That's an ore cart, right? Modified?"

"That's how it looks to me."

"So they probably have never taken it out before. Maybe once they get this electrical connection or whatever sorted, they'll be underway."

"Fair enough. But still, a hundred and fifty klicks, more or less, sitting on that thing. That's going to be at least five hours. And I'm guessing much longer. Quite the trip."

"Not one I'd want to take. Desperate times, I guess."

"They should just talk to us," Tasha said. "We would have given them haven. Of some kind. Maybe they would have had to deal with the legal implications, but at least they'd be safe and warm."

"Like I said, desperation. They ain't gonna trust us."

"I suppose not."

Ed kept looking at the display with the zoomed in view. One of the three was just standing watching Ed and Giselle's buggy approach. The other two were working on the vehicle.

"Perhaps we're missing something," Ed said. "What if there is something nearer? Something we don't know about."

"We know about everything," Giselle said.

"We didn't know about this mine until their ship exploded."

"Good point. Sorry."

"Tasha," Ed said. "Can you have the computer parse historical data on the region? Say, a hundred klicks out from the crater wall. South east direction. Maybe there's something there."

"Do you think there will be?"

"It's just one possibility. Maybe they've called in uplift, but need to get to a specific landing site? Perhaps they were going to swing around the crater rim and come back up to us? It's pretty hard to make a determination just because they headed in that direction."

"Agreed. But I'm running the looksee now, find out what the data can tell us."

Over all the long decades of examining the lunar surface, there were databases that were just vast with imagery and arrays of thermal, seismic and other data points.

Running the system to analyze the area shouldn't take a

whole lot of resources. And it might show something up. Perhaps even a recent landing plume from a launch vehicle.

Ahead, the small group were remounting their vehicle. Giselle and Ed's buggy had closed to within five hundred meters. Soon they would be ascending the rocky slope.

"Hey," Ed said. "Also thinking about the explosion. Did we run an analysis on the data on that?"

"I did," Tasha said. "Mostly it was seismic. Nothing visual."

"But now we should also wind back. Figure out when that mine was established."

"I'll do that. Once we've run the analysis on your projected area. See if they are actually headed some place."

Ahead, the other vehicle started moving again. More slowly now, though likely it would pick up speed.

"We might catch them," Giselle said. "We have momentum for the slope, and we won't lose much speed."

"But there's no way to know the specs on that vehicle, though. A repurposed ore cart."

"Yep. Those things trundle along pretty slow, but I guess you could goose the motors and turn the cart into a racecar."

How would you do that? Put a couple of the motors in series? Maybe regear them? That would seem to be the most likely.

They had had a couple of days to work on things since that rocket had exploded. Perhaps Ed finding the line of the ramp door at the moment they drove out was just a coincidence.

Or perhaps they'd been frightened into leaving before they were ready.

Which could be why their vehicle had broken down.

Not broken down now, though. Now it was powering away and picking up speed.

Giselle and Ed's buggy was on the slope now. Perhaps just

two or three hundred meters behind. Making good time, but slowing as the angle sucked away their momentum.

"Do we have ranging on it?" Ed said.

"Two hundred eighty meters," Giselle said. "We're closing the gap. They're not as fast now. Not on the slope."

"We might catch them on the other side? Once we're over the summit of the pass."

"Summit of the pass," Giselle said with a laugh. "You make it sound like we're on a road into Tahoe, not on the barren, life-less face of the moon."

"Yep." Ed smiled. He tapped at his console display and tried to bring up the ranging himself. It took a couple of goes, but he got it. The buggy's sensors fed back a simple linear radar bounce to give a distance.

Two hundred sixty-eight meters.

Closing the gap. But slowly.

Still, they had to follow.

"I have data," Tasha said.

"Go ahead."

"So it looks like there is a facility much closer. It's still around sixty kilometers from your current location. The activities noted suggest that there was a mine operating there as recently as three years ago. No official records, and little surface evidence."

"No one thought to go look?" Giselle said.

"It's only now that we're looking closely at the area that the details are coming up. There's nothing there alone that would stand out. Only when we compile, as we're doing now."

"Makes sense. Do you have a heading for us?"

"From where you're going to come through the gap in the crater wall, you'll want to bear off at around one six five degrees."

"South, south east."

"Kind of. I can track your progress from here and give you any course corrections."

Ahead, the ore cart with the welded-on seats crossed the summit and slipped over the other side out of view.

Into the darkness.

"How's our juice?" Ed said. "For traveling, what, four hours in the dark?"

"You'll be fine. Your buggy's little reactor is burning away nicely. You're fueled up and ready for a month out in the dark, if that's what it took."

The buggy was a pretty top of the line model really. Clean and new and with running gear that was extremely well maintained. Ed knew the specs were high, but he hadn't realized that it could run through the lunar night.

"We won't need a month," Giselle said. "Sunrise will be in two weeks."

As she said it, the buggy crested the rise and started down after the other vehicle.

The darkness was complete, save for a single bright beam that cut through it.

The ore cart. Lighting the way for itself.

"We follow?" Giselle said.

"Yeah, we do."

Ed peered into the darkness.

He'd never been any great distance away from a base during a lunar night before. This could be interesting.

CHAPTER FOURTEEN

The ore cart was running rough. Claude could feel it.

They'd barely even left the mine and the cart had broken down and Stacey hadn't been able to fix it quite right.

The vehicle shuddered and shook. If it had been in atmosphere, the sound would have been just awful. The mechanism grinding against itself.

Sixty klicks of this. Just great.

He peered ahead into the gloom. The big mine lights shone out across the rough landscape. Flat in places, covered in rocks in others. Off to the left, at the blurry edges of the light spill lay what might have been an old rille.

A billion years old. No *four* billion years old.

From when the moon had still been molten, with a just-hardening crust. Little rivers of lava had flowed along, leaving the rilles—empty streambeds in effect.

One of the big lights guttered and died.

The darkness seemed to sweep in. With a kind of enthusiasm.

All of this was starting to feel like a bad idea.

He kind of just wished he'd stayed back at the mine. He could have sipped at their meager supplies of hot chocolate and just waited.

People had discovered them, so he could have been rescued. It would have meant interviews with the authorities, and quite likely some jail time, but right now a nice warm secure jail cell sounded better than sitting on a claptrap modified ore cart traipsing off into the lunar dark.

"Light?" he said.

"Yeah," Stacey said. "Looks like it's shorted or something. Don't worry, we have a couple spares in the trailer. And I'm feeling as if I only need one to be able to see where we're going."

"You can see all of thirty meters ahead. We could drive off a cliff before you could stop."

"Don't worry, this baby stops fast."

"And I'll go flying off."

"Oh. Right. We'll take a break soon. I'll figure out making you some kind of harness. Maybe just with some cord that we've got back there."

"Great," Claude said. "Just great."

"Do I hear sarcasm?"

Claude didn't respond.

He pulled himself around to look back. The equipment tossed into the trailer jostled around, tied down with cord. The trailer was just another ore cart, but still with its high-sided ore tray.

Farther back, the other vehicle was still following. Bright headlights cut through the massive darkness.

Much closer, but perhaps falling behind.

The ore cart and trailer were picking up speed.

Maybe Claude could just jump off and wave down the other vehicle.

Would it make his situation any worse, really?

"Stop soon," Emanuel said. "Make the harness now."

It was as if Emanuel was kind of on his side.

"If I stop," Stacey said, "they'll catch us. Claude, whyn't you just climb over onto the trailer and find the cord. Fashion yourself a harness from it. Or just tie yourself in."

Claude looked at the linkage between the two ore carts. Just the standard fist and knuckle set up from the mine. Strong as anything, but likely if he put his foot on it he would slide off.

Then he would fall. Land under the wheels of the trailer.

That would make a real quick end to things.

"Yeah," he said. "I might just wait it out."

CHAPTER FIFTEEN

E d held his console display close as Giselle drove the buggy deeper into the darkness.

Tasha had sent through details on the mine. The one towards which they were heading.

It had been operating illegally, and shut down when it got discovered. Enough safety violations to make even Ed blanch.

"We're just three hundred meters behind them now," Giselle said. "They're not moving so fast."

"But still faster than us?" Ed looked up.

The darkness was near-complete. Stars, of course, and off to the right, near the horizon, the Earth half in shadow and half bright. Over the next week it would grow gibbous, then full, before waning once more.

The last thing puncturing the dark was the light from the other vehicle. Shining out across the lunar surface.

"Still faster," Giselle said. "But not by much. They lost some power there."

"So we can almost keep up, but we won't catch them?"

"Correct."

"For sixty kilometers?"

"Hard to say. We'll possibly lose them soon."

The lunar horizon lay around two kilometers off. The surface's curvature was almost visible. If the other vehicle was moving just five kilometers an hour faster, then it would disappear inside of half an hour.

"Any way we can raise them?" Ed said. "Any luck with the radios?"

"Nothing," Tasha said. "The ground ahead of you is somewhat hillocky, though. They'll be going up and down. You'll lose sight of them next time they crest a hill, but then when you reach that same point, you'll be able to see farther. Probably pinpoint them too."

"Helpful."

"And current tracking shows them heading straight toward that abandoned outpost. They will have to make right and left detours around some of the hills and boulders. This is relatively flat land too. Lucky we're not on the far side."

The moon's far side—the side that permanently faced away from Earth—lacked mares like Oceanus Procellarum. The surface was far more cratered and broken up.

"Solutions?" Ed said. "Are we monitoring incoming vessels now? Perhaps they've called someone in for an exfil."

"Let me check. There is a lot of traffic around."

Lunar space had gotten busy over recent years. Some of the new techniques were making it so just about anyone could launch from their back yard and land themselves on the moon. There was money to be made and adventures to be had. Not quite at the tourist levels that had overwhelmed some Earth cities for years, but still somewhat cluttered and chaotic.

That was part of what seemed to allow the wildcatters some free rein.

"Okay," Tasha said. "There's nothing in the vicinity without proper clearance, and nothing that looks likely to make a landing in your area any time soon. Could be, though, that there is a ship that's on track to set down at the other location in a day or so."

"How do you mean?"

"Might just change their flight path. Last minute."

"Right."

The thing was that even if these folks did make a getaway, it wouldn't be clean. They could easily be tracked, now that the system knew what it was looking for. Simple enough to put eyes on the ship's location and simply follow it wherever it went.

Chances were, that would be back to Earth.

But all that took resourcing. Satellite time. People time.

Easier to pick them up on the ground.

Assuming that Paladan station allowed them the resources to continue the pursuit.

Technically this formed a training mission, really. And Ed was out here in training.

Trekking out into the dark like this was a real test. The buggy could handle it, but there were numerous other issues to consider.

"Four hours?" Ed said.

"Looks that way," Giselle said. "More or less. And most likely not less. With the terrain and the dark, we need to be vigilant."

"Copy that."

Ed peered ahead. There was minimal reflection from the forward window's internal face.

The Moon's surface was ragged and blocky. Smooth dusty

areas punctuated with rocks and cracks and smaller meteor craters.

If a grain of sand impacted the surface it would leave a crater here. With the kinds of velocities involved, of course. Tens of thousands of kilometers per hour. Would make a bullet look like a slowpoke.

"You want to go in back and rest up a while?" Giselle said. "I've got this for now. Maybe switch out driving in a couple of hours?"

Ed glanced at the airlock hatch in the rear of the cab.

"Tempting," he said. "But if we catch them, I need to be ready too."

"We're not going to catch them."

"Their vehicle might break down again."

"Fair point."

"I'll observe," Ed said. "I can take over the driving later. You're better at it than I am, anyway."

"I know it."

Ed leaned back.

This could turn into a long night.

CHAPTER SIXTEEN

C laude saw the shift in the topography perhaps a half a second before Stacey did.

A drop away.

As Claude opened his mouth to shout, Stacey was already braking and turning.

The ore cart's brakes were good. The sudden deceleration threw Claude forward. He grabbed hold of the backs of the two forward seats.

Almost went flying through.

But the braking and turning wasn't enough.

Stacey had been running the very edge of the cart's speed, but pushing the limits of what she could actually see ahead.

She was turning left.

The right front wheel went over the lip. Into darkness.

The whole cart tipped up. Shuddered.

Emanuel yelped.

Claude tumbled around behind Emanuel. Claude scrambled to grab at something. Anything.

But then he was off the cart. Falling.

Still with all of the momentum from the cart's headlong rush across the surface.

He fell away.

Emanuel lurched out. Grabbing for him. Still strapped to his seat.

Their hands touched. Claude grabbed.

But he was done.

Too late.

Their fingertips brushed past each other and Claude dropped away into the dark.

CHAPTER SEVENTEEN

E d watched as the cart made a sudden left turn. It tipped.

"Uh-oh," Giselle said.

"Yep."

The cart was a good four hundred meters from them. Ed watched the video coming through on his console display in the buggy's cab.

Zoomed in.

The ore cart had found a hole in the darkness. Maybe a simple rille, or perhaps a low-walled crater.

"They're off-balance?" Giselle said. "Going to roll?"

"Teetering," Ed said. "But they've got that trailer hooked up. It looks as if that's keeping their center of gravity well back."

"Driving too fast."

"Think so. Trying to keep ahead of us."

"So now it's our fault?"

"Ha, ha."

"If they come to a stop we should be with them in a couple of minutes."

"I don't think they're stopping."

The ore cart had kind of righted itself. It was still moving forward. Slowly. Heading toward the left. Driving on around whichever obstacle it had encountered.

"Tasha," Ed said. "Do we had clear maps on this area?"

"I can send it right though to your console there," she said. "I think we have down to ten centimeter resolution."

"That'll do it. Tell me, is there a hole there? Perhaps a lava tube opening?"

"No opening. There is a small scarp. Geology indeterminate."

"Small?"

"Four meters."

"Yep. Wouldn't want to drive over that any time."

"Nor me," Giselle said.

The map appeared as an icon on Ed's display. He tapped to open the map up and the icon swelled to fill the whole display. Right away the buggy's system loaded in its location and heading.

"Slow up a little," Ed said. "Feel as if we're at risk of going over too."

"I'm tracking for them," Giselle said. "How far along does this scarp go? We might be able to head them off soon."

Ed looked up. The ore cart was still going to their left. Heading north east.

On the console, he zoomed the map out a fraction.

"A kilometer," he said. "It just kind of blends back into the regular surface level."

"Give me a heading. We can cut them off."

With a couple of taps, Ed brought up a route. Tapped between the two points.

"Heading one six two," he said. "From now."

The buggy made a slight correction left. The motors hummed and the chassis rocked.

"Hey," Ed said, brain finally kicking in with when he'd glanced up at the ore cart.

He looked again.

Was one of them missing?

He focused again on the console display. He brought in the video feed again.

There were only two of them sitting on the ore cart now. One of the occupants was gone.

CHAPTER EIGHTEEN

Claude lay back in the dark, the wind knocked out of him.

A quiet hissing came from somewhere in his helmet.

He gasped, trying to get a breath.

In. Out. In. Out.

There were stars above him. Bright. Sparkles.

But all around him, on the ground, there was just darkness.

When he caught his breath, he sat up a little. A tiny alarm was sounding in his suit. Was that life support?

He'd landed on his back. Right down on the ground.

Lunar falls weren't so bad, what with the low gravity, but they were still falls. And with his own weight combined with the suit's weight, he had plenty of mass.

He looked up. He could see where the edge of a cliff cut off the starscape.

How far had he fallen?

He didn't see the ore cart.

"Guys?" he said.

Nothing. The hissing continued.

"Hey?" he said. "Stacey? Emmanuel? Where are you?"

Instinctively he reached to turn on his suit lights, but this was just an old jalopy of a suit. No lights. Slapped together with resin and paste and straw matting.

"Emmanuel?"

Claude rolled around onto all fours and pushed back so he could stand. Whole different techniques for being on the lunar surface in a suit.

On his feet, he looked around.

He might as well have been standing in a pool of ink.

He took a step. Couldn't even see his feet.

A shiver ran through him. Not cold.

Fear.

"Emanuel?" he said. "Please come in."

Nothing.

Line of sight comms. That was the best he could hope for.

Claude tipped back a little to follow the line of the cliff. Impossible to tell how big it was.

Couldn't be that high. Anything above about thirty meters and he would have been killed outright.

Probably less, even.

He took another step. Into the darkness.

The hissing continued. Was he losing suit pressure?

He held his hands out in front of him. Reaching for the cliff face.

If he had to climb, that would take forever. At least, it would take longer than the time he had before the sunset.

On the moon, the sun took an awful long time to go down, but still, it had only been a matter of hours when they'd left the mine.

He glimpsed a light. Off to his right.

Was that the ore cart? It seemed a long way off.

"Emanuel?" he said. "Stacey?"

"Hey—laude. You do—all—ite?" Emanuel's voice was clipped and broken.

"I'm okay," Claude said. "Might have punctured my suit. Can you guys get to me? Maybe lower a rope. A cord."

"We—natch—"

"Did not copy your last," Claude said.

"—then—"

The light from the ore cart faded out.

"Emanuel?"

Nothing.

"Emanuel, please. Please respond."

But there was still nothing.

They'd left him.

Left him in the dark on the moon.

CHAPTER NINETEEN

In the buggy's cab, Ed ran back through the footage of the ore cart when it had made the sudden turn.

He slowed the playback down.

It looked as if one of the wheels had gone over the edge. The whole contraption had jerked and tipped. The person in the rear seat had not been strapped in.

They'd gone over the edge.

Vanished into the dark.

And the ore cart had kept on driving.

"One of them bought it," Ed said. "There are only two of them on the ore cart now."

"Bought it?"

"Fell off. Out here, that's nasty. Hey, bear right again. Heading, one six eight."

"Huh?"

"Let's go look for this one."

"He'll be dead. If he fell at that speed. Over a four meter scarp."

"Maybe. But let's recover the body. We're not going to catch up with the other two anyway. And getting this one will help any investigation."

And there was always an outside chance that they had survived.

"Understood," Giselle said. "Our bearing is now right for where he vanished."

"Perfect."

"So you're letting the others go?" Tasha said through comms.

"How do you think the tracking is going on them?"

"Just fine. We've got six eyes watching. And also someone's running the variables on all the vessels in local space in case one of them veers off to make a pick up."

"I think we're good, then. Let's go grab this miner and see what they have to say for themselves."

"Assuming they're alive," Giselle said.

"They made it."

"You're always very hopeful. I like that about you."

Giselle focused ahead. She adjusted something on her console and a strobe light started up, flashing out into the dark, giving them flashes into the distance.

It momentarily threw the scarp's near edge into sharp relief.

CHAPTER TWENTY

Claude's hand bumped into something. The cliff's face. He stopped.

Looked along in the direction where the ore cart had vanished. With Stacey and Emanuel.

Abandoning him.

A shudder ran through Claude.

There was no way out of this.

Dead man walking.

The hissing from his suit continued. He was losing air.

Rather than hours of life left, he had perhaps minutes.

If he had a decent suit, it would have had a Heads Up Display that would have given him all kinds of details about the suit's status. He would have had a patch kit, which would have helped if he could reach the puncture. He would have had lights that would at least let him see into the Stygian dark.

He looked up. The starfield was cut off sharply by the edge of the cliff. So hard to tell how high it was.

Couldn't be all that high, right? Not if he'd survived the fall.

If he could get himself to the top, he would be back in sunlight. Even if briefly.

That would be a better place to die.

Another shudder.

With his right hand, he felt around for a grip in the cliff's face. Climbing in the dark. What a ridiculous activity. No way to see any handholds. It would all be by feel. With thick old suit gloves and chunky, ridged suit boots.

He felt across the face. Found a niche. Dug his fingers in.

They slipped out right away. He stumbled back.

Fool's errand.

And the was clearly the biggest fool of all.

But standing here wasn't doing anything about helping himself.

He reached again. Felt around. Found a protrusion. Gripped it. Pulled himself up on it.

Moved his right foot. Managed to get it into some kind of hollow.

Reached up with his left hand. Felt around for ages. There was nothing there.

Perhaps he'd already found the only two irregularities in the cliff face.

There. Another protrusion. Bigger than the first.

He pulled himself up. Got his left foot against something.

Thank goodness for the low gravity. Even with the suit, the one-sixth gravity at least made the climb a little easier.

The hissing continued. Disconcerting.

Claude reached. Pulled himself up again. Stretched and pulled.

He kept finding hollows and knobs to pull himself up on.

Hey. He might even make it.

Around him light flashed.
Claude jerked. Lost his grip.
Fell.
He grabbed at the cliff face.
Didn't get any kind of grip.

CHAPTER TWENTY-ONE

Ed clambered down from the buggy's cab. Giselle had parked them ten meters back from the edge of the scarp. The strobe had shut off now.

"Tethers," Giselle said, coming around from her side, carrying a length of coiled cord. Two lengths. She handed one to Ed.

They quickly tied themselves into the little automatic winches on the buggy's nose. The winches would let them walk around, keeping just enough tension on the cords, but would lock up if any sudden movement was detected. Such as from falling over the edge.

Ed walked with purpose. He had his suit lights blazing and he carried a handheld flashlight.

"I see the wheel marks," Giselle said. "Looks to me as if they were lucky not to take the whole caboodle right on over the edge."

"Caboodle?"

"It's a technical term. It means a hastily thrown together repurposed item with no aesthetic value."

Ed smiled. Even in a situation like this, Giselle could still sometimes show a sense of humor.

Walking on, Ed shone his flashlight right at the edge. One of the wheels had indeed gone right over. They had indeed been lucky not to lose the whole caboodle.

Ed looked along to the left. The light of the makeshift ore cart was distant now. Hard to say how far off. Perhaps two kilometers. The dark was growing as the sun continued its slow descent.

He looked back the way they'd come. The rim of Serenda crater stood out rough and stark. The sun was just touching the rim. Very soon, this whole area would be draped in darkness.

Reaching the scarp's lip, Ed chose his footing carefully. No sense in slipping and falling, even if he did have the tether. And who knew how friable the edge might be?

Giselle kept pace with him, just a meter or so to his left. They came up to the edge together.

Absolute blackness stretched out in front of them. A kilometer or so off, a rolling, smooth peak stood up high enough to catch the last of the sun light. Stark and bright.

But between them just lay a sea of night.

Ed and Giselle both shone their flashlights down into the abyss.

The ground was peppered with rocks and boulders. Dusty regolith lay spread out all around.

The scarp's face was irregular, with pits and lumps.

And there, almost directly below them, someone was free-climbing the face.

CHAPTER TWENTY-TWO

Claude reached again. Grabbed at a knob. He'd gotten farther on this second attempt at scaling the cliff.

But he was starting to feel light-headed.

The hissing had gotten quieter. All sorts of factors in that. Lower air pressure, so the sound wasn't carrying so well. Lower air pressure also meant that there just wasn't as much air going through the hole.

In the darkness, he reached for another handhold.

Wouldn't it be just the thing to get almost within reach of the top of the cliff and find that there were no more handholds?

That would just be his luck holding on at about the same level as the last couple of hours, and the last few days, and, well really, the last few years.

There was light again. Not the brilliant flare that had startled him and caused him to fall. This was a different kind of thing.

Like pendant light swinging just above him. The light kind of flickered onto his arms. And onto the rock face.

He could see.

Another handhold there. And another little crack in the rock over there.

He stretched. Grabbed.

Pushed up.

The light was coming from above. He tipped his head back to look, but the top of his helmet stopped him from seeing past the rock wall.

He needed to use it to his advantage. Who cared where it came from? Didn't matter.

Another handhold. And another.

He was making progress.

Almost at the top.

He reached, and grabbed at a protrusion.

It broke away in his hand.

Claude felt himself tipping back. Again.

He knew that his suit wouldn't take another impact.

This was it.

CHAPTER TWENTY-THREE

E d had seen the suited figure climbing.

No ropes. No safety mechanism of any sort.

Just meter or so from the top.

"I'm going down the face," Ed said.

"How?" Giselle said.

"Walking. Running. Make sure the tether doesn't lock up on me."

"Copy that."

Ed leaned out over the scarp's edge. The tether's tension held him.

He started walking down. Keeping to the figure's left.

"Can you hear me?" Ed said.

No response.

"I've got their signals now," Tasha said. "It's all running on a pretty primitive encryption system, but I can't break it."

"So they might be receiving?"

"Potentially. We're government public domain, so nothing we say can be encrypted at all."

"Right." Ed kept walking down the scarp's face. Held in place by the tether.

"Attention climber," he said. "I don't know if you can hear me, but if you can, stay put. I'm going to come down and pull you up."

The person reached ahead again. Grabbed at a rocky knob.

Ed walked faster. This was a maneuver he'd practiced. Once. At a climbing wall in Atlanta. Just a single day's training. With a whole bunch of other equipment and people around helping.

And the rope had been around him, running through carabiners so he could manage his rate of descent, and so that if he slipped, the rope would lock off and he wouldn't fall.

He had to trust the buggy's winch system to do the job here.

"Attention climber," Ed said as he came parallel with them. "Stop climbing. I'm going to grab you now. I'll tie you off."

The person grabbed again at the rock face. Hoisted themselves up. Pretty confident. And probably they would make it unassisted, but that thought didn't make Ed comfortable at all.

He took another step. Searched around the waist of their suit, looking for a tie point or a ring. Something he could use to harness them in to himself.

There wasn't really anything. The suit looked pretty old and done in.

Giselle's lights flicked across Ed and the climber.

"How are you making out down there?" Giselle said.

"Don't know how I'm going to tie them—"

Ed broke off as the climber fell back.

Instinctively Ed lunged. Grabbed at the arm as it whipped by.

Then the climber was falling away.

CHAPTER TWENTY-FOUR

Claude's stomach clenched as he fell again.

Dropping down the cliff face. His mind whirled.

Even light-headed as he was.

Probably he was going hit it somewhere and then he would be tumbling and spinning.

And then he would land on his head.

And that would be that.

But then he came to a sudden stop.

He swung around.

Upside down.

Bile rose in his throat. He tried to choke it down.

Wouldn't it be funny to drown in his own vomit after all of this?

He giggled.

Was that hypoxia? Lack of oxygen? Was that even what it was called?

But he felt warm. Felt a nice soft blanket wrapping him.

So this was what it was like to die on the moon. Alone and in the dark.

Perhaps he was all right with that.

He let the darkness come.

CHAPTER TWENTY-FIVE

E d got a hold of the climber's boot.

"On my way," Giselle said, before Ed could say anything.

"Wait up," Ed said.

"You need me. You can't maneuver him like that. I'm coming down with clips and more tether."

She was right. Ed had a grip on the astronaut's heel but that was it. If he moved, likely the person would slip and slide on down the scarp.

Moments later Giselle was right there.

The climber had his back against the wall. Ed was on his knees facing down.

All of them dependent on the tether, which, Ed suddenly realized, was scraping against the rock at the top of the scarp.

The tether was tough, though. He shouldn't even worry about it.

Just needed to get this person to safety.

"Stay right where you are," Giselle said. "I'll clip them off."

"I don't see any tie points."

"There are always tie points."

"You're thinking in terms of regulations, not wildcatters."

"I've already found one."

"I stand corrected."

Ed could feel the person slipping. Even with just a one-sixth gravity, Ed's grip on the boot wasn't that secure.

"I'm losing them," Ed said.

"I'm working on it here."

"You should grab hold too."

"Then I can't manage the carabiners."

"Hurry."

"Stop saying that. I need to focus."

But Ed was definitely going to lose his grip.

"Grab them for a second," Ed said. "Let me regather my grip."

"Okay, I'll—"

The boot slipped anyway.

Out of Ed's grasp.

CHAPTER TWENTY-SIX

Hanging from the tether over the edge of the scarp, Ed lunged again.

Grabbed with both hands.

Got hold of the person's leg. With both hands.

"Hold on," Giselle said.

"You bet."

Ed saw her reaching.

But then he was falling too. His tether whipped in front of him.

Pinging away with the release of tension.

Clearly not up to the job of sliding over a rock edge.

"Ed!" Giselle said.

"I'm here," he said. "I'm okay."

He still had hold of the person's boot. They had swung around and were now dangling from their waist.

Giselle had clipped them in.

"Question now, though," Giselle said, "is how we get the both of you up."

"Can you climb back up, still on your tether?"

"I can."

"Then get up there. Run another tether through like a block and tackle on the edge to keep it from running against the rock."

"And you'll hold on the whole time?"

Ed did his best to look around. Below him lay just black darkness.

"It doesn't look too far to fall."

"Nope," Tasha said from back at the station. "I have eyes on you from overhead. Looks to me as if your feet are no more than forty centimeters from level ground. Just watch you don't turn an ankle as you land."

"Copy that."

"Then Giselle can send you down another line and you can climb back up."

"That will work," Giselle said. "Give me a couple of minutes."

"Great," Ed said. "I do not like the idea of hanging from the person's boot. Looks to me as if the whole suit could fall apart any moment."

"Copy that."

"And that would disastrous for them. I might get bumped around a bit, but..." Ed trailed off.

"Ed?"

"Get them up safely."

"What are you doing."

"It'll be all right."

Ed let go of the boot.

CHAPTER TWENTY-SEVEN

As he fell, Ed crouched.

It wasn't far to the bottom. And lunar gravity being what it was, he wasn't falling fast.

But he still had the weight of his suit and life support pack.

And he could still land awkwardly.

Giselle was yelling in his ear. Fortunately the helmet's speakers attenuated the volume so it was only her vocal expression that came through and not how loud she probably was being.

She would damage her own ears with the sound echoing around in her helmet.

Ed hit the bottom.

Yep, awkwardly.

Right foot down first. Then his left. He stumbled.

Stood on a loose rock that rolled and tipped him over.

He landed on his right side.

His suit lights went out.

Telltales flickered orange in his helmet.

Ed came to rest.

The helmet telltales quickly returned to green. He hadn't done damage to the suit.

"Giselle," he said. "I'm on the ground. I'm all right."

"Sheesh, man," she said. "Know how to give me a fright or what?"

"Is our person safe?"

"Winching them up now. Then I'll come get you."

"I'm all right. Get them into the buggy. I'll wait for you to send me a rope."

Giselle's response came after a hesitation.

"Copy that," she said.

Ed stood. He left the suit lights off.

Around him was nothing but dark. As if someone had gotten blackboard paint and coated the entire moon. No. It was more than that. It was a complete and full darkness. As if the shadows were sucking up every last speck of light. Like a black hole.

Ed looked up. The Earth hung there, bright and shining at him. Australia stood partly in darkness as the sunrise crept its way toward Perth. And there were stars too. Filling the sky.

If he waited a while, his eyes would grow used to the dark, surely, and he would begin to see features on the ground, slightly illuminated by the sun's reflection from the Earth.

He took a deep breath. Took a sip of sweet juice from the helmet's drinking straw.

It was surprisingly peaceful. The only sounds were the quiet hum of his life support pack and the little helmet fans.

Fascinating. He was here on the moon. In the dark. Isolated and alone.

He could be the only person out here.

It was oddly disconcerting, but also oddly comfortable.

Here under the stars.

He didn't get many moments like this.

And, even though distracted, he couldn't really take one now.

"Giselle?" he said. "Progress?" Ed swung around and looked up the scarp's face.

The person in the suit was almost at the top. Giselle was standing above, working on the tethers.

Almost there.

"I've about got them," Giselle said. "What's your status?"

"Fine to wait down here."

"I don't see your suit lights."

"They shut off in the fall. I kind of like it down here in the darkness, though."

"Oh yeah?"

"Ed," Tasha said from back at the station. "Turn on your lights. Giselle needs to be able to see you."

"Copy that."

Ed turned them on, but a moment later, Giselle had the person up and over the lip.

He stood for a moment looking up at the face of the scarp. It was an unusual feature on the moon, but Ed had learned not to be surprised. Despite excellent mapping, most of the moon still lay unexplored on foot. There was always something new to find.

The scarp's face was sheer, with few handholds. Talk about chutzpah, that person taking on climbing up it. Especially in the dark. In a suit.

Ed was looking forward to talking with them. Resolving this, but seeing what kind of person they were.

Turning, Ed shut off his lights for a moment. Just to enjoy the intriguing isolation.

The universe seemed huge from his perspective right now.

A vast, wide void, ready to explore.

"Hey," Giselle said, breaking into his thoughts. "What are you doing? Tasha told you to turn on your lights."

Assuming, correctly, that he'd turned them off intentionally.

"Yeah," he said. "Should I be worried that I like the darkness?"

"Definitely. We'll get you into therapy when you're up here. Speaking of which, our guy is back in the buggy, so if you'd like to join us, well, I'm tossing a rope down the scarp."

"Thanks, then. I'll be right with you."

And he stood for another moment, lapping up the night.

CHAPTER TWENTY-EIGHT

It was cramped inside the buggy's habitation space with three of them.

Ed managed to strip out of his suit to help Giselle with their new arrival.

Claude. Claude Halbert.

The man had been barely coherent. Freezing cold. Only just able to walk back to the buggy. Giselle had had to just about drag him along. Once she'd gotten him inside and out of his helmet and she'd felt confident that he would survive, she'd hustled back to get Ed.

"How is he?" Ed said.

"His suit lost a lot of air, but he'll make it. No embolism or lung damage that I can see. Looks like we got him just in time, though."

Claude lay on one of the bunks. Eyes closed. Breathing evenly.

"And the others?"

"Tasha's tracking them now. Looks as if their ore cart has

actually broken down. They're working on it, but Welman Base is sending over a hopper loaded with some supplies and a tent. Should allow them to wait it out until someone can get to them."

Claude stirred.

"Were they ever going to get away?" he said.

"Nope," Giselle said. "I mean, I'm impressed with the ingenuity, and I realize that when your ship exploded it left you in a bad position. But you all should have just called for help."

"I would have liked to. Am I going to jail?"

"Not up to us." Giselle looked over. "Is it Ed?"

"We're just glad that we were able to get you out of a sticky situation," Ed said.

"Likewise," Claude said. "And anyway, jail would be better than the muck hole I've been working in." He tried to sit up. "Who are you people?"

"Stay lying down," Giselle said. "There's not much room there." Reaching in, the rapped her knuckles against the underside of the top bunk, just a few centimeters above Claude's head. Space was at a premium inside the buggy.

Claude lay back. "Thanks for pulling me out of there," he said.

"All part of our friendly service," Ed said.

"Friendly's good. I haven't had much of that lately." Claude sighed. He shivered. "What happened to the others? Stacey and Emanuel?"

"The vehicle broke down," Giselle said. "Another team is on the way to pick them up. With more space in their vehicle than we have here."

Claude nodded. "They're not bad people. They've just ended up in a bad situation."

"Understood. Like you?"

Now Claude snorted. "Hardly matters, does it. We're the

ones who got caught. Honestly we're lucky to be alive. When the *Enchanted Whimsy* blew up, I thought that was it. Thought I was dead."

"Could have been," Ed said. "We were close. But now we'll take you back. You hungry?"

Claude nodded.

"I think we have some granola bars around. Something like that."

"We do," Giselle said. "But we'll have a decent feed once we get back to Paladan."

"Sound good?" Ed said.

"You bet."

"All right then. Giselle, you want me to drive?"

"If you would. I'll feed this man and let him get some rest."

"Great." Ed squeezed around to the airlock hatch and patted the mattress beside Claude. "Good to have you safely here."

"Why are you being so nice to me?" Claude said.

"What?" Giselle said.

"I'm not supposed to be here. Our operation was illegal. You know that. But you're being good to me. Food and a bed and, well, pulling me out of that hole. You could have just left me out there."

"You're a fellow human being," Ed said. "Here on the moon. That's enough for us."

Claude blinked and looked as if he was about to cry.

"Hey," Giselle said.

"I just... I just..." Claude took a gasp.

"Listen," Ed said. "We're all explorers and travelers out here. No matter the circumstances, we've got to look out for each other."

Claude nodded.

Ed patted the mattress again and slipped through the airlock.

The cab's external doors were sealed, so the airlock could stay open, making the whole buggy open space.

Ed nestled into the driver's seat and brought the motors online. He settled the headset on and let Tasha know that they were on their way back.

"I heard," she said through the headphones as Ed engaged the drive and started them back around. Heading toward the cleft in the crater wall.

"You heard all that?" Ed said.

"Matter of public record, in fact. You were way too nice to him. The expenditure of resources over these people is ridiculous. The two of you. The vehicle. Now the other hopper flying in. It'll affect budgets."

"But people are alive," Ed said. "That's what matters, isn't it? Out here. We all have to look out for each other."

"Yes," Tasha said with a kind of resigned sigh. "Yes we do."

"We'll see you soon."

Ed lined up on the crater and drove them on, heading toward the slowly setting sun.

AFTERWORD

I've written elsewhere about how, when I wrote the adventure novella "Wildest Skies", I discovered that there were other Ed Linklater stories to tell in that world of galactic exploration and astronaut training.

"Wildest Skies" itself is really the fulcrum of the series. To my suprise, it found itself on two ballots—for the Sir Julius Vogel Award, and the *Asimov's* Readers' Poll, in 2025. It was gratifying to have it so well-received.

Meanwhile, though I kept on telling more stories. Some (like this one) are set before the events of "Wildest Skies", and others are set after. It seems they are building up a broader narrative of Ed Linklater as he trains and grows as an astronaut both on either side of the life-changing events on Dashel IV.

Also, after "Landing Protocols", this is, I believe, the second story to include Giselle Mäkinen. She's a fun character to hang out with as I write the stories. A good foil, I think, for Ed and his impetuous nature.

There are more stories coming with Giselle as the lead character. One, "Gate Torus" is near completion and I hope to have it out in the near future. (Note, I'm not promising— not when a story is 'near completion'. It's better to wait until the story is *actually* complete before making grand pronouncements. With best intentions and all the will, life's little hurdles can sometimes slow things down.)

But "Gate Torus" will come out, as will other stories. I have fun writing these, but it's almost as much fun getting them tidied up and ready for publication, making a cover and even writing these afterwords. I hope that these give some small insight into the writing process.

Thanks for reading. I appreciate it. Feel free to stop by the website and say 'hi'. It's always good to hear from Readers.

Sean
September 2025

ABOUT THE AUTHOR

Award-winning author, Sean Monaghan has published more than one hundred stories in the U.S., the U.K., Australia, and in New Zealand, where he makes his home. A regular contributor to Asimov's, his story "Crimson Birds of Small Miracles", set in the art world of Shilinka Switalla, won both the Sir Julius Vogel Award, and the Asimov's Readers' Poll Award, for best short story.

He is a past winner of the Jim Baen Memorial Award, and the Amazing Stories Award.

Sean writes from a nook in a corner of his 110 year old home, usually listening to eighties music.

www.seanmonaghan.com

instagram.com/seanmonaghanauthor
facebook.com/seanmonaghanauthor

ALSO BY SEAN MONAGHAN

OTHER WILDEST SKIES STORIES

Spindle Shatters

Shards of Tempered Glass

Martian Job Offer

Choppy Waters

Designation One Eight Nine

———

CAPTAIN ARLON STODDARD ADVENTURES

Asteroid Jumpers

Ice Hunters

Ship Tracers

Core Runners

Desert Creepers

Underworld Climbers

Island hoppers

Mist Drifters

Dead Ringers

Tramp Steamers

Cradle Robbers

Margin Dwellers

CAPTAIN ARLON STODDARD Shorts

Ortanide Steppers (novella)

Sea Skimmers (short story)

Dark Behemoth (short story)

KARNISH RIVER NAVIGATIONS

Arlchip Burnout

Canal Days

Eastern Foray

Guest House Izarra

Jackpot Kingdom

Liquid Machine

Night Operations

Persephone Quest

Rorqual Saitu

Tombs Under Vaile

Waxing Xebec

Yesterday's Ziggurat

THE JUPITER FILES

Book 1: Deuterium Shine

Book 2: Tritium Blaze

STANDALONE SCIENCE FICTION

The Ergs

Raphael Marooned

Hanging Vines

Raven Rising

Athena Setting

The City Builders

The Cly

Gretel

SCIENCE FICTION SHORT STORY COLLECTIONS

Balance

Balance II

Balance III

*Un*Balanced

Listen, You!

OTHER COLLECTIONS

Arms Wide

One Degree Below Freezing

Landslide Country

STANDALONE THRILLERS

The Courier

Ice Fracture

Rotations

Taken by Surprise

EMILY JADE SERIES

Big Sur

Glass Bay

COLE WRIGHT THRILLERS

The Arrival

Measured Aggression

Hide Away

Slow Burn

Scorpion Bait

Concentration

CONTEMPORARY NOVELS

This is the Perfect Way To Wake

Steel Wagons

MORGENFELD

The Mapmaker of Morgenfeld

The Stairs at Cronnenwood

The Chimneys in Atterton

The Wintermas Paintings

The Bergeron Sculptures

The Ingersal Ballet

www.ingramcontent.com/pod-product-compliance
Lightning Source LLC
Chambersburg PA
CBHW020917180626
46816CB00007BA/2450